For Freya, Love from David

To Amy, Love from Stephen

A Doubleday Book for Young Readers

Published by
Random House Children's Books
a division of
Random House, Inc.
New York

Doubleday and the anchor with dolphin colophon are registered trademarks of
Random House, Inc.

Text copyright © 2004 by David Almond
Illustrations copyright © 2004 by Stephen Lambert
First American Edition published 2005
Originally published in Great Britain in 2004 by Hodder Children's Books,
a division of Hodder Headline Limited

Visit us on the Web! www.randomhouse.com/kids
Educators and librarians, for a variety of teaching tools, visit us at
www.randomhouse.com/teachers

Library of Congress Cataloging-in-Publication Data is available upon request.

ISBN: 0-385-74691-1 (trade)
      0-385-90929-2 (lib. bdg.)

MANUFACTURED IN CHINA
October 2005
10 9 8 7 6 5 4 3 2 1

Kate, the Cat and the Moon
David Almond and Stephen Lambert

A Doubleday Book for Young Readers

Once, in a shining night,
while the moon looked down
and the stars glittered in the endless sky,
and all the house was lost in dreams . . .

. . . the little girl called Kate woke up and heard a cat.
"Meow," called the cat. "Meooow!"

Moonlight fell across Kate's face.
A million stars glistened in her eyes.
"Meow," called the cat from the night.
"Meow. Meow. Meow."

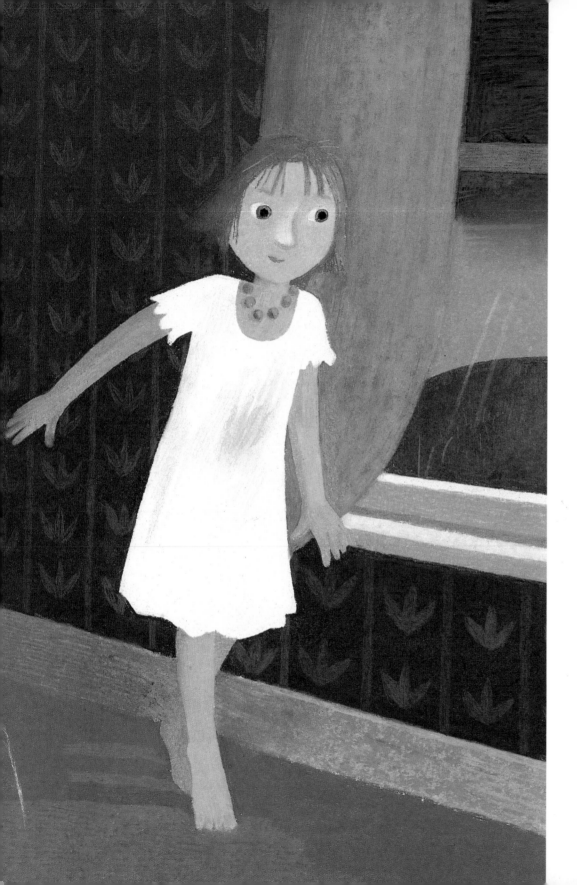

Kate tiptoed to the window in her
white nightdress.
The cat was on the garden wall.
It licked its paws.
It stretched its neck.
It swung its tail.
Its coat shone, as white as the moon.
It turned its starry eyes to Kate.
"Meow," Kate whispered.
"Meow. Meow!"

Kate smiled as she changed.
She touched her pointy ears.
Out of the bedroom, over the landing, down the stairs.

Jump,

jump,

jump,

jump!

She licked her tiny sharp teeth
with her tiny rough tongue.
She lifted her paw to her face
and felt the whiskers growing there.
She felt her smooth soft coat.
She scratched her claws against the floor.
She licked her paws
and stretched her neck
and swung her tail.
"Meow," she called. "Meow!"
And her voice was high and wild
and strange.

She listened.

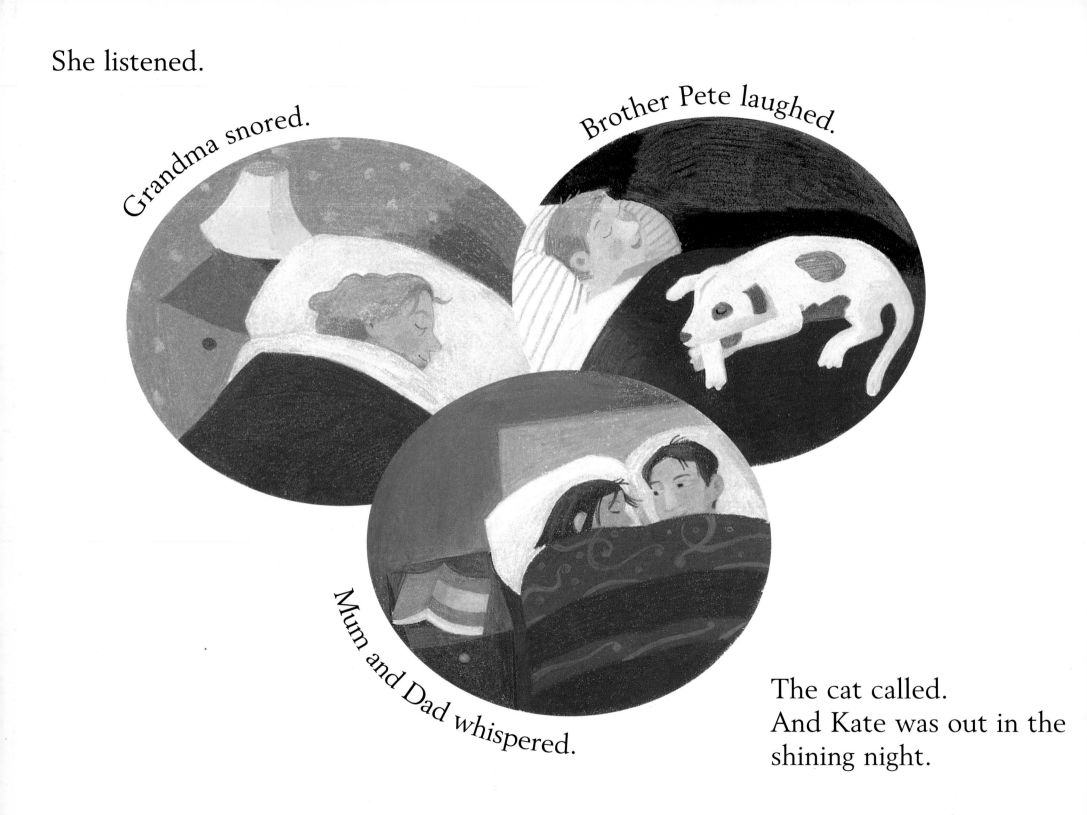

Grandma snored.

Brother Pete laughed.

Mum and Dad whispered.

The cat called.
And Kate was out in the
shining night.

Through the shadows of the garden,
through the silvery light.
She stopped beneath the garden wall.
Two cats together
in the shining night
as the moon looked down.

Off they went, into the night . . .

Past dreaming houses, shady gardens,
through pitch-black lanes,
down broad pavements,
under burning streetlights,
over empty roads and massive bridges,
past the edge of the town,
through hedges and ditches
and into the fields.
Jump, jump, jump!
To a little hill with a stony top.

"Meow," they howled.
"Meooooooooow!!"

The moon looked down.
It licked its tiny sharp teeth
with its tiny rough tongue.
"Meow," it called. "Meow!"

And all the sky was full of dreams. . . .

Back through the fields,
the hedges and ditches,
over the bridges and roads and pavements,
back beneath the burning streetlights,
through pitch-black lanes,
past dreaming houses and shady gardens
and back to the garden wall.

The stars went out.
"*Meow,*" said the cat.
"*Meow,*" said Kate.

Flap, *click*, *clack*, stop.
She listened.

Across the landing,

Up the stairs, jump, jump, jump!

into the bedroom,

into bed.

She closed her eyes
and went to sleep. . . .

Next day the talk was all of dreams.
"We walked by Heaven Lake," said Mum and Dad.
"I chased Patch through Butcher Street," said Pete.
"And I danced all night long with Grandpa at the Roxy!"
"Did you dream, Kate?" they asked.

"Meow," said Kate. "*Meow.*"